Dear Parent:
Your child's love of reading starts here!

Every child learns to read in a different way and at his or her own speed. Some go back and forth between reading levels and read favorite books again and again. Others read through each level in order. You can help your young reader improve and become more confident by encouraging his or her own interests and abilities. From books your child reads with you to the first books he or she reads alone, there are I Can Read Books for every stage of reading:

SHARED READING
Basic language, word repetition, and whimsical illustrations, ideal for sharing with your emergent reader

BEGINNING READING
Short sentences, familiar words, and simple concepts for children eager to read on their own

READING WITH HELP
Engaging stories, longer sentences, and language play for developing readers

READING ALONE
Complex plots, challenging vocabulary, and high-interest topics for the independent reader

ADVANCED READING
Short paragraphs, chapters, and exciting themes for the perfect bridge to chapter books

I Can Read Books have introduced children to the joy of reading since 1957. Featuring award-winning authors and illustrators and a fabulous cast of beloved characters, I Can Read Books set the standard for beginning readers.

A lifetime of discovery begins with the magical words "I Can Read!"

Visit www.icanread.com for information
on enriching your child's reading experience.

Library of Congress catalog card number: 2013947667
ISBN 978-0-06-211076-3 (trade bdg.)—ISBN 978-0-06-211075-6 (pbk.)

14 15 16 LP/WOR 10 9 8 7 6 5 4 3 ❖ First Edition

Pete wants to look cool.

He asks everyone,

"What should I wear?"

"Wear your yellow shirt,"
his mom says.
"It is my favorite."

So Pete does.

"Wear your red shirt,"
Pete's friend Marty says.
"It is my favorite."

So Pete does.

"Wear your blue shirt,"
Pete's brother Bob says.
"It is my favorite."

So Pete does.

"Wear your long pants,"
Pete's teacher says.
"They are my favorite."

2+2=4

So Pete does.

"Wear the shorts with the fish,"
Pete's friend Callie says.
"They are my favorite."

So Pete does.

"Wear the polka-dot socks,"
the bus driver says.
"They are my favorite."

So Pete does.

"Wear the cowboy boots,"
Grumpy Toad says.
"They are my favorite."

So Pete does.

"Wear the tie with the stripes,"
Emma says.
"It is my favorite."

So Pete does.

"Wear your baseball hat,"
his coach says.
"It is my favorite."

So Pete does.

Pete puts on all the clothes.

Does he look cool?

No.

Pete looks silly.

He also feels very hot!

Pete goes home.

He changes his clothes.

Pete puts on HIS favorite shirt.

Pete puts on HIS favorite pants.

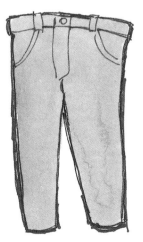

Pete puts on HIS favorite socks.

Pete puts on HIS favorite shoes.

Pete puts on his sunglasses.

Pete says, "Now I am COOL."

If you want to be cool,
just be you!